First Heroes for
FREEDOM

by Marcia Bjerregaard

Illustrated by Marty Jones

SILVER MOON PRESS
NEW YORK

For information:
Silver Moon Press
New York, NY
(800) 874–3320

Library of Congress Cataloging-in-Publication Data

Bjerregaard, Marcia.
First heroes for freedom / by Marcia Bjerregaard ;
illustrated by Marty Jones.--1st Silver Moon Press ed.
p. cm. -- (Adventures in America)
Summary: A fifteen-year-old slave is sent to join the Continental Army in
America's war for independence, the outcome of which is either death
or freedom from slavery.
ISBN 10893110-17-6
1. United States--History--Revolution, 1775-1783--Participation,
Afro-American--Fiction. 2. Slavery--History--Fiction.
I. Jones, Marty, ill. II. Title. III. Series.

[Fic]--dc21

10 9 8 7 6 5 4 3 2 1
Printed in the USA

To the slaves and freemen of
Rhode Island's Black Regiment
who fought for their freedom,
and ours.

— MB

To Judy, with gratitude—
for trusting God enough,
and trusting me enough,
to say 'Yes.'

— MJ

ONE

TWO HORSES PULLED THE WAGON AT A jerky trot along a rutted lane of Aquidneck Island. Fifteen-year-old Cuff sat miserably, stuffed between two cloth sacks, long dark arms clutching knees to his chest. He wanted to forget what he had just seen, but he couldn't help looking back toward Newport. Heavy black clouds of smoke hovered above the town before the sea breeze blew them toward the retreating wagon. Even here, three miles away, Cuff could smell burning wood. In his mind he could still see the British soldiers bashing in windows of houses and chopping at sheds with their axes.

"Cuff, I'm sorry about the Beckhams," the driver called back to him. Cuff turned and glanced at Mr. Barker's back. Isaac Barker, in his mid-twenties, wore his brown hair pulled into a twist that hung at the nape of his neck below his wide-brimmed hat. His gray shirt gathered at the neck with a little collar and loose sleeves. Cuff wore the same kind of shirt—one of Mr. Barker's old ones—but his was ripped on one sleeve.

"I'm sure they've left because of the fighting," Mr. Barker continued, voice tight. Cuff could tell he was upset too. "I just hope your family is safe."

"I do too," Cuff said, biting his lip. He felt certain that if the Beckhams had gone, they would have taken his father, mother, and little brother with them. After all, as slaves, they were part of the Beckhams' property and had been all their lives. They wouldn't leave their property behind, would they? Cuff had also been born on the small Beckham farm, but on his tenth birthday Widow Beckham sold him to Mr. Barker for a good price. Now, the Beckham property, like many other farms, had been looted by British soldiers.

For almost two years, the British had occupied Aquidneck Island. The island was long and narrow, protecting the waterways that led inland. By positioning themselves here, the British had stopped all sea trade and commerce from reaching Providence, Rhode Island's main city.

Cuff crawled over several sacks to lean on the back of the wagon seat. "Do you know where they might have gone?" he asked weakly. "They probably headed north to Howland's Ferry," Mr. Barker said. "That way they'd have a chance of reaching the mainland. I'll see what I can find out. Perhaps my brother knows."

"Yes, sir," Cuff said, biting his lip so hard that he could taste blood. Cuff had always liked it when Mr. Silas Barker, who lived on the mainland, rowed across the Sakonnet River in his boat to visit. Silas liked to laugh and tell jokes. He hadn't visited them in months, not since a British colonel and his troops set up camp on the Barker's farm.

The wagon slowed down as it neared the Barker's property. Paradise Farm sat at the foot of Barker's Hill, the highest hill on the south end of the island. The hill itself was like a small mountain, its top covered with blue-gray rocks that turned purple after it rained. Down on the farm, the soil was rich and thick enough for vegetables to grow in the fields, and enough grass covered the hill for sheep to graze. That spring, Cuff had put in a garden for Mrs. Barker, with herbs and flowers, near the two-story shingle house. Susie, the cook and housemaid, cooked with the herbs and Mrs. Barker cut the flowers.

"The British are doing terrible things," Cuff said, expecting Mr. Barker to agree with him. When Mr. Barker was silent, Cuff knew he should have kept his opinion to himself. Ever since the British had moved onto the farm, Mr. Barker had been acting strange.

"They're getting ready to fight to hold the island," Mr. Barker finally answered, looking over his shoulder. "They're burning everything in front of their battle lines so the Continental Army won't have anything to hide behind during an attack."

The wagon lurched over a deep pothole, and Cuff fell back into the wagon bed. As he righted himself between a sack and the wooden side, he remembered hearing that the Continental Army was going to combine efforts with the French Navy to drive the British off the island. He'd been unloading baskets of beans at the British fort at Green End at the time.

Six days earlier Cuff had seen the French Navy, ten ships cruising in from the Atlantic, fire cannons at the anchored British ships. The British had been so surprised they hardly shot back. In an attempt to avoid capture and to block the western waterway leading to Narragansett Bay, the British burned and sunk five of their own ships. That didn't stop the French Navy from sailing into the bay. And they were still there. At the same time, two other French ships sailed up the Sakonnet River, just east of Barker's Hill. Cuff had heard the cannon fire and watched as Mr. Barker climbed to the top of the hill to see what was happening.

"They've damaged British ships at Fogland Point," Mr. Barker had announced when he came back to the house. Minutes later, several more explosions filled the air. The next day they had heard that one of the British ships had caught fire and blown up from the ammunition on board. After that, Cuff was sure the British would surrender, but they didn't.

Cuff considered the British the enemy because they had ruined so much of the land. But he knew there were others on the island who sided with the British. In fact, he was beginning to wonder if Mr. Barker was one of them. Before the British colonel and his Hessian troops—which Mr. Barker had explained were from a place called Hesse-Haupt in Central Europe—came to Paradise Farm, Cuff used to overhear Mr. Barker complaining to his wife about the British lords who ruled the colonies. But the Barkers didn't speak about the subject much any more. Mr. Barker seemed different now.

The wagon turned into the yard of the Barker farmhouse, which sat between the dirt road and the fields.

Tall hickory trees kept it shaded all summer. As Mr. Barker stopped the wagon under one of the trees, Mrs. Barker emerged from the house carrying their two-year-old daughter in her arms. She looked worried.

"Are you all right?" she asked her husband as he climbed down from the wagon. She wore a plain gray dress with long sleeves. A white apron hung over her skirt, and a small white cap with drawstrings covered her light hair. "I saw the smoke. Was there fighting?"

"They're burning farms, barns, houses . . . everything!" Cuff said anxiously.

"All right, Cuff," Mr. Barker reprimanded. "Now take the wagon to the barn and settle the horses."

"Yes, sir," Cuff said, embarrassed by his outburst. But still—Mr. Barker should have been more upset.

"Susie has your noon meal waiting, Cuff," said Mrs. Barker. "Come to the house to eat when you're done there."

"Yes, ma'am," Cuff mumbled.

"Big changes are coming, Sara," Cuff heard Mr. Barker say to his wife, as they headed toward the house.

Big changes are already here! Cuff thought, slapping the lines along the horses' flanks to get them moving. His family was missing, the farm he grew up on was in ruins. He hoped nothing else changed too soon.

After settling the horses, he was heading across the yard toward the house when he heard a voice calling. "I say! You, boy. Come here!"

Cuff turned to see the British colonel who'd been living on the farm. The colonel, wearing a powdered white wig and dressed in white breeches with a red coat, beckoned to him with the hat he held in his hand. In his other hand he held a riding crop. Realizing that the colonel had probably just come from Newport, Cuff stayed where he was, clenching his teeth. This man had probably given the orders to burn the town.

"Come here, I tell you!" the colonel repeated.

Reluctantly, Cuff shuffled over to him.

"Get on down near the orchard to my officer's tent," the colonel ordered. "He needs his riding equipment cleaned and clothes brushed out."

Cuff wasn't sure how to respond. After all, he couldn't refuse an order from a white man. "If Mr. Barker allows," Cuff finally said, wondering if Mr. Barker had told the colonel it would be all right. "But I have work to do in the fields." He stared at the ground, unable to look the colonel in the eye.

"Why, I've given you an order, boy!" the colonel said, angrily.

"What's going on here?"

Cuff sighed with relief as he heard Mr. Barker's voice coming toward them. He didn't dare take his eyes off the ground.

"I need your boy, here, to help my officer," the colonel said to Mr. Barker.

"I'm sorry, Colonel," Mr. Barker said calmly. "He can't today. He has work to do in my fields." Cuff felt Mr. Barker's hand on his shoulder. "Go on to the house and get your dinner, Cuff."

"Yes, sir," Cuff replied, wishing he could run to the house before the colonel could convince Mr. Barker to change his mind. He could hear the two men arguing as he crossed the yard. Susie was standing at the door frowning, her gray-white hair tied up with a dark green cloth. Susie, once a nursemaid to Mrs. Barker, was now an old woman. But despite her age, she did all the household chores and cooking.

"Things sure have changed since that Redcoat arrived," Susie said, as she led Cuff into the kitchen. She handed Cuff a tin plate of mutton with bean stew, a thick piece of bread, and a wooden spoon, before returning to peer out the open door. Cuff sat beside the hearth on a three-legged stool and began to eat. Susie wasn't as good a cook as his own mother, but the food was filling. Unlike some farm arrangements, the Barkers and their slaves ate the same food.

Through the kitchen window, Cuff noticed Mr. Barker and the colonel walking toward the house.

"So how much more trouble do you think the rebellious colonists will be?" he heard Mr. Barker say through the open window.

The rebellious colonists? Cuff repeated to himself. Could Mr. Barker really be siding with the British?

"Ah, the rebels," said the colonel. "Their plans won't mean anything once Admiral Howe arrives with reinforcements. Clinton is sending more Hessian troops and extra battleships."

"The rebels won't have a chance," Mr. Barker chuckled. "Even with their French allies." Mr. Barker's friendly tone made Cuff scowl. He had always looked up to Mr. Barker, who had been considerate and kind. He made sure Cuff saw his family the first Sunday of every month and he often talked to him as if he were a son, not a slave. But lately, everything had changed.

"So I need the boy's help in the fields if I'm to keep fresh vegetables going to your troops down at Green," Mr. Barker was saying.

"All right, Barker," the colonel said, gruffly. "But I still suspect you're afraid he'll run off and join up with my forces. Or haven't you told him he could get his freedom by fighting with the British?"

"He is working for the British," Mr. Barker insisted. "Helping to feed them, at least."

Susie backed into the kitchen, shaking her head. "You don't have any ideas about becoming a Tory, do you Cuff?" she asked, chuckling.

"No, ma'am!" Cuff said, shaking his head. "Even if the British hadn't burned the place I was born and raised, I wouldn't chance it."

Cuff had heard about what happened in 1775. Lord Dunmore, the British head of the Virginia Colony, had proclaimed that if slaves fought for the British they'd be set free. The slaves who believed him escaped from plantations in the south to join the British. Soon after, several of them came down with smallpox and, when the British were forced out of the colony, were left behind. The men who survived the illness had no choice but to return to their angry owners.

Cuff heard the colonel's heavy footsteps on the wooden floor of the drawing room that he'd taken over as his own. Cuff finished his dinner hastily, so he could head out to the fields, anxious to get as far away from the colonel as possible.

TWO

AS CUFF HOED WEEDS FROM THE CORN-field behind the barn, the August sun grew hotter and hotter. After a couple of hours, he decided to take a break on the top of Barker's Hill where there was always a cool breeze. As he climbed the steep slope, he realized that he hadn't been to the top for a while, though it was his favorite place on the property. When he reached the gate at the top, he could see the sheep grazing in the pasture below.

He looked down at the water of the Sakonnet River, a quarter mile down the rocky slopes on the opposite side of the hill. Across the river he could see Little Compton's beach on the Rhode Island mainland. The British hadn't bothered to post troops there. At other times he had seen men working on ships near Flint Point, to the south. If the day was clear, he could actually count the cannon spread out below the Union Jack flags. *But no ships are there today, thanks to the French*, Cuff thought. He felt a shiver run down his spine when he saw the smoke still billowing from the burning farms near Newport.

He looked toward the north, where he hoped his family had gone with the Beckhams. *Where were they?*

He wondered. Had they taken Bristol or Howland's Ferry to the mainland? He couldn't see the ferries, both of which were twelve miles away. All he saw were thick woods on Quaker Hill in Portsmouth, about eight miles away. Mr. Barker had friends on Quaker Hill, and Cuff had joined him on several hunting trips there.

"Cuff!"

Cuff turned and watched Mr. Barker stride toward him, his face flushed from the steep climb. "I told you not to come up here!" Mr. Barker scolded. "Not for any reason!"

Cuff cringed. "I'm sorry, sir," he apologized. "I forgot." Now he remembered. A few weeks earlier Mr. Barker told him that the hill was off-limits. Usually he remembered what he was told, but all the worry about his family had distracted him. "I was taking a short break and just wanted see if the French—"

"Sorry is no good." Mr. Barker said, shortly.

"Yes, sir," Cuff mumbled, looking at his feet.

"You usually follow orders quite well," Mr. Barker said, placing a hand on Cuff's shoulder. "Listen carefully, you are always to do what I, or Mrs. Barker, ask of you without question. We're trusting you to that."

"Yes, sir," Cuff managed. He felt shaky inside, dreading that Mr. Barker would order him to work for the British colonel. "I won't come up here anymore."

Boom. Boom. Boom.

There was a sudden thumping of cannons in the west, where Cuff saw battleships heading out to sea. Every time a cannon fired, smoke rose from the shore.

"It looks like the French Navy is leaving!" Cuff said, alarmed. Without the French, who would keep the British out of the harbor?

"So it appears," Mr. Barker said, with a scowl, staring hard at the sea. Then he turned toward Cuff and changed his tone. "All right. Get on with you, then. There's more hoeing to be done. Then the tool shed needs to be straightened, and the hoe blades need sharpening."

"Yes, sir," Cuff replied. He reluctantly started down the hill. He wished he could have stayed and watched what was happening. He turned back one last time and saw Mr. Barker pacing back and forth near the fence.

*   *   *

That night Cuff awakened to a whisper.

"Cuff. Cuff, wake up."

When he opened his tired eyes, he found Mrs. Barker staring at him, her fretful child in her arms. Mrs. Barker often walked her young daughter in the cool yard during the summer, but she had never before come to the barn where Cuff had his cot. Susie stood behind Mrs. Barker holding a candle and a small knapsack.

"Cuff, listen to me," Mrs. Barker whispered. "You're to do just as I say."

"Yes, ma'am." Cuff sat up and rubbed the sleep from his eyes.

"Tonight you will run away from here," Mrs.

Barker said. "You'll join up with General Washington's Continental Army."

"Ma'am?" Cuff was both surprised and frightened by the order; his heart began to thud.

"After what happened with the colonel today," she said, "we think it best that you go."

"But—" Questions were flooding Cuffs mind, but he knew it wasn't his place to ask them. "I . . . I don't know how get to the mainland," Cuff said, clambering to his feet.

"You don't have to," Mrs. Barker said, shifting her daughter to her other hip. "The Patriots are up north by Portsmouth."

"The Continental Army is on this island?" Cuff asked with awe.

Mrs. Barker nodded. "After the French showed up, the British brought most of their forces closer to Newport. That's how the Americans were able to take over the fort on Butts Hill." Mrs. Barker looked around suspiciously and then leaned close to Cuff. "Listen well," she whispered. "You're to take the old sheep path down to the shore and then go up toward Sandy Point. From there you can take the East Road. There probably won't be any British guards."

Cuff nodded. East Road began in Newport, running up toward Mount Hope Bay.

"Here's a few loaves of bread, a woolen bedroll, and a few other things you might need," Susie said, handing Cuff the knapsack. Mrs. Barker handed him a piece of folded parchment, sealed with a dollop of wax. "Give this letter to Major Samuel Ward,"

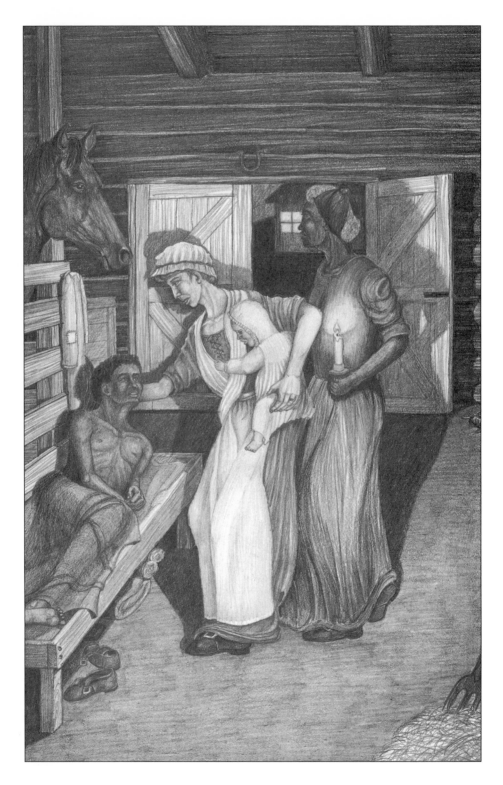

she said. "Hide it in the knapsack under the bread."

The baby started to whine. "Shhh." Mrs. Barker gently rocked her daughter. "I must go back to the yard. Good luck to you, Cuff. You'll always be in our thoughts." She hurried away with Susie at her side, carrying the candle.

For a moment, Cuff stayed where he was, clutching the letter in his hand. You are always to do what I, or Mrs. Barker, ask of you without question, he remembered Mr. Barker saying that afternoon. But go all the way to Portsmouth, by himself, in the dark? Did Mr. Barker know about this or was Mrs. Barker working against her husband? *Always do it without question,* he remembered.

Swallowing hard, Cuff buried the letter under the loaves in the knapsack, pulled on his high socks and boots, and flung the knapsack over his back. He eased quietly out the back door and looked for a moment at the dark barn and the Barker's house. Then, without turning back, he crept across the cornfield and around the old sheep pen, not making a sound. He had no idea what would become of him, but that was no reason to turn back.

THREE

AS CUFF WALKED ALONG THE OLD SHEEP
path, he was grateful for the light from the half-
moon above. Though it was a relatively quiet night,
Cuff was aware of every type of sound: an owl hoot-
ing, crickets in the grass, a raccoon hunting. He
hoped no soldiers were stationed on this side of
Barker's Hill. He held his breath at a cracking
sound in the tall sticker hedge and froze for a full
ten minutes. It turned out to be another raccoon.

A few minutes later, he reached the shoreline and
followed it toward Sandy Point. At the ferry landing
he crouched behind some hedges and peered across
the river. Despite the moonlight, he couldn't see
much. All he heard was the lap of water against the
bank. *Maybe I'll wake up and find this was a dream*,
Cuff thought, wishing he were in his bed in the barn.
But his feet hurt too much for it to be a dream. He
took Fogland Road west to East Road and then
turned north. Suddenly he realized that this was the
way the Beckhams might have gone. He tried to
imagine his father carrying his sleepy brother over
his shoulder while his mother walked beside them.
They would have traveled at night too.

He walked through a wide valley covered in farmland. The low stone walls surrounding the farms made him nervous. What if someone were hiding behind them? Anyone might pose a problem for Cuff. It wasn't as if he were free. He could be sent back to Mr. Barker, who probably didn't know he was gone. But maybe he did know. Maybe Mr. Barker had sold him to the Continental Army for 120 pounds. That's what the Rhode Island Assembly had promised to pay owners for the service of their slaves. At least being sold to the army was better than being forced to work for the British. He began to walk faster, hoping to avoid being out in the open when dawn came.

As Cuff walked past a wheat field, startled rabbits thumped through the grass. He neared Lawton's Mill, the mid-way point, and stared up at the huge windmill looming stark and eerie in the fading moonlight, its great white blades twirling slowly in the early morning air. He shivered and hurried on. A flock of birds flew overhead, squawking in the graying sky.

Before long he came to the white Quaker meeting house with brick chimneys at each end. As Cuff climbed the slope of Quaker Hill, he noticed that the farms showed very little damage from the British. Aside from a broken window and a trampled garden—both of which anyone could have caused—the farms were in good shape.

It can't be too much further, he told himself, his feet aching. The road sloped upward through thick, dark woods. When he reached the top of Quaker

Hill he headed right back down the other side, into a small valley. Not another hill! Just as he started to climb, he heard footsteps. Heart pounding, he scrambled for a place to hide.

"Stop right there!" ordered a deep voice.

Cuff turned and found himself facing a long musket. It was pointed right at him! He put up his hands until he saw that the man holding the musket was wearing a blue coat—a Continental soldier! Cuff sighed with relief. *I've made it!*

"I've come to enlist in Mr. Washington's Army," he said.

"That's General Washington, boy," the soldier said. "And we can't take any runaways."

"I'm not a runaway, sir," Cuff explained. "My mistress sent me. She told me to give this letter to Major Samuel Ward." He pulled the letter out of the knapsack. Though he didn't know how to read it, he was sure it would tell who his owners were. Otherwise, how would they know who to pay . . . that is, if he were right in assuming Mr. Barker had sold him to the Continental Army.

The soldier studied him a moment and then called toward the woods. "Private Potter, come escort this man to camp."

"Yes, sir," came a reply, and Cuff was surprised to see a slender, black youth step forward. He looked only a bit older than Cuff, perhaps seventeen.

"My name's Nat Potter," the young man said, beginning a brisk pace through the silent woods. "Your master sent you to join the army, huh? He must have a son he doesn't want to send to the militia."

Militias were separate from the Continental Army. They were formed by volunteers from the colonies, who agreed to fight for three to six months. Instead of uniforms, militia members wore their own clothes, used their own guns, and were free to go home if they wanted to.

"No," Cuff replied. "All he has is a young daughter. In fact, it was the Missus who sent me here." Walking uphill didn't seem as bad now that he had company. Cuff caught up to Nat. "So you're a real soldier?" he asked. "A private?" Nat nodded. "What's it like being in the army?"

"It's a lot of hard work, that's for sure," Nat said.

"I'm used to hard work," Cuff said, "but do you have to fight?"

"We haven't had to yet, but I'm sure it will happen soon," Nat said.

"Who is Major Ward?" asked Cuff. "Mrs. Barker said I should give this letter to him, but I have no idea who he is."

"He's one of the officers in charge of the First Rhode Island Regiment," Nat replied. "That's the regiment I'm in. You'll be joining it too if Major Ward okays you. Most of the men in it are black, and if we make it through this war, we'll all be free men. We'll be able to do as we please for the rest of our lives."

"Really?" Cuff said, hardly able to believe his ears. "It seems strange that I'd get sold to the army to fight for my freedom."

Nat shrugged. "That's how it is. I can't wait till

I'm a freeman. I'm going to buy a piece of land and build my own house and grow my own crops and no one can ever tell me what to do again."

Cuff wondered what he would do if he were free. He had been a slave all his life—someone else's property for as long as he could remember. "If I were free I'd go find my family," Cuff said, with new hope. "I'd want to live with them or near them. They're not free." He wondered if the Beckhams would pay him to work for them so he could be near his family.

As the sun began to shine through the trees above, they came to a clearing. White canvas tents dotted the hillside, with glowing, orange cook fires around them. Soldiers went in and out of the tents, some moving barrels and crates.

"Look at all the people!" he exclaimed. "I never imagined the fort would look so much like a . . . "

"Like a city?" Nat asked, laughing. Cuff nodded.

"That's because there's thousands of men. Last week, the British left so fast they didn't take the time to wreck everything the way they usually do," Nat said. "Even the battery mounds and powder rooms were still intact." They stepped aside as an ox-drawn wagon pulled a cannon past them, then passed through the outer defenses of the fort area at the crest of the hill.

Seconds later they came to a big, square-sided tent with an awning out front. A man in uniform stood outside. Nat saluted the man, who was Major Ward's aide, and then explained Cuff's situation. Cuff handed him the letter that had been buried under the bread in his knapsack. The aide disappeared into the tent and returned with Major Ward, a tall, strong looking young man. His face was spotted with shaving soap and his white stockings hadn't yet been pulled up over his breeches.

"What's your name, lad?" he asked Cuff, wiping his face with a towel.

"Cuff, sir." Cuff stood as straight and tall as he could, hoping to make a good impression.

"And your farm?"

"Paradise Farm."

"I know the Barker place," Major Ward said, nodding. "Add 'Cuff Barker' to the roll of the First Regiment!" he ordered his aide. "And find him a tent and provisions." He handed Cuff a piece of paper with the Continental Army seal on it.

"Sir! There's space in my tent," Nat spoke up.

"Fine, fine then," Major Ward said. "You can help him get settled."

"Yes, sir!" Nat said, saluting.

Cuff imitated Nat's salute. He wondered if he was dreaming. Even though he wasn't free, this sure felt different from being a farm slave.

As soon as they were out of earshot, Nat pointed to the piece of paper Major Ward had given him. "That's the contract with the army—and your freedom paper. When you get out of the army, you carry that with you and nobody can make you do anything you don't want to do ever again."

Cuff gazed at the piece of paper with awe. He could see the writing on it, but couldn't read the words. "When I get out of the army, I'm going to learn to read," he said.

Nat grinned, "Me too, but there's a lot more to do before then." He bent down and picked up a piece of a tree limb about as long as his hand and as wide as his arm. "If you plan to eat, you'll have to carve out your own trencher."

"Sure," Cuff said. His father had taught him how to carve a trencher when he was younger.

"This afternoon I'll give you a haversack with other things you'll need: a canteen, a tinderbox, a ration of bread," said Nat. "Sometimes we get cheese from a nearby farmer but—I have to warn you—it's often as hard as a rock."

The tent was empty when they arrived. Cuff counted five bedrolls.

He spread out the bedroll Susie had given him to make six. Nat gave him a shirt and a pair of white leggings that went down over his shoes called overalls. "We weren't expecting any more recruits, so the boots you're wearing will have to do for now."

"Thank you," Cuff said. He couldn't believe he was truly a part of the Continental Army. He yawned, suddenly exhausted from the long journey and the little sleep that he'd gotten the night before.

"Why don't you rest," Nat said. "You've come a long way. I'm going to lie down too, since I was on night duty. I have to march in a review this afternoon. I'll wake you up then."

Although he was tired, Cuff found it hard to sleep. His mind was racing with all that had happened in just one day. He tried to picture his family, safe and sound at the Beckhams' new lodgings. Did his father's back still ache? Did his mother still sing while she sewed? Did his younger brother still sleep with his thumb in his mouth? He hoped he was right in thinking they were safe. If they weren't . . . it was too painful even to think about. He hoped the war would be over soon so he could find his family. He reached into his knapsack and pulled out his contract with the Continental Army. *Soon I'll be free*, he promised himself before drifting off to sleep.

FOUR

CUFF AWOKE TO SOMEONE SHAKING HIM, "Hey, Cuff." Nat's face came into focus. "Wake up. I've got to march, but first I want to show you something." Cuff's eyes still felt heavy, but he quickly dressed in his new shirt and overalls—the first new clothes he had ever owned. He guessed he was going to have to get by on less sleep now that he was in the army.

"Here, I forgot to give these to you this morning," Nat said, handing Cuff a tomahawk and a straw hat. "I'm sorry to say that the army is out of muskets, too, and we're not sure when we can get more. I'll train you on mine once you've gotten the hang of every-thing else. While I'm at it, here's your haversack with the rations."

"Thanks," Cuff said, taking the haversack and admiring the light ax.

Nat led Cuff to the highest edge of the hill. The mid-afternoon sun was hot. Cuff was grateful for the straw hat. All the men were wearing them. "Look down there," he said, pushing aside some branches.

Cuff looked down and saw hundreds of men busy at work, unloading food, ammunition, cannons, and horses from flatboats on the beach of the Sakonnet River. Men were also feeding horses, repairing carts, and cooking food. On the far side of the bay, away from the smoke of the fires, officers' shirts were spread on the bushes, drying in the sun. "I guess there's lots of plain ol' work to this soldiering," he said.

"Yep, they're working mighty hard down there, and I was too. Look over there," Nat said, pointing toward the mainland. "That's Tiverton, where I worked for Major Talbot. I helped build those flatboats."

"That's pretty impressive," Cuff said, looking with admiration at the sturdy looking flatboats tied up along the shore.

"Yesterday, those boats ferried ten thousand men and supplies across the river from the new fort at Tiverton," Nat explained. "Some are borrowed, but we built eighty-six of them. We had to do it fast to replace the flatboats the British burned."

"We'll have those British whipped in no time!" Cuff exclaimed.

"Especially with the French helping," Nat said. "They're supplying four thousand more men. With us on land and the French on the sea, it should be easy to drive the British off. We have to do it fast, though. British ships are blockading Providence, and the people there are stuck with no food. Meanwhile, the British are helping themselves to everything here on the island . . . vegetables, cows, sheep. Even butter and milk from families with children. It's a good thing island folks sent most of the food to the mainland. That helps us and hurts the British."

"Well, it sure did make them angry," Cuff said, remembering one of Mr. and Mrs. Barker's conversations. "Some of the farmers who were smuggling food to the mainland got caught. The British filled their wells with dirt and tore the wheels right off their wagons."

"That's awful," Nat said. "Did it happen to your master?"

Cuff shook his head. "Nat, something's been bothering me about Mr. Barker. The British are constantly stealing from folks, or breaking their things and burning down homes. But they never bother Mr. Barker."

"That's odd," Nat said, chewing on a long piece of grass. "Why do you think that is?"

"Mr. Barker has a British colonel living right in his house," Cuff said, relieved to be able to talk to someone about his suspicions. "And he gives meat and vegetables to the Hessian regiment camped on his farm. The colonel even gave him a pass saying he can travel around the island."

"He must be a Tory," Nat said. "A Loyalist."

"That's what I figured," Cuff said, "but why would he sell me to the Continental Army?"

Nat shrugged. "Your Mr. Barker sounds strange. It doesn't make any sense to me either," he said, standing up. "But come on. We better go, so I'm not late for the review. Make sure you watch so you know how it's done. Soon you'll be marching yourself." They went down the hill to a big field where the men were assembling. Cuff sat and watched on a nearby slope under a large walnut tree. Even though he was out of the sun, it was awfully muggy. Still, it was a grand thing to see nearly 130 black men walking proudly in unison, their muskets propped on their shoulders. *They look like free men already*, Cuff thought, admiring the energy and spirit with which they moved.

As the other regiments took the field, he noticed that most of the soldiers wore overalls like the ones he had been issued. Others wore knee breeches and tall boots. The officers all wore fancy uniforms with lots of brass buttons: on the vest, on the jacket, lining both sides of the front, ringing the cuffs, and holding open the flaps on the back. The blue coats also had red, green, or gold braid on the shoulders, and a few were embroidered with stars. Everyone wore uniforms, even the drummers. A man sitting near Cuff told him that the most important responsibility of the drummers was to relay battle orders. Cuff noticed that a few of the musicians looked younger than he was. Soon he could pick out the different drumbeats, watching with interest as the soldiers changed formation with the latest rhythm.

Cuff continued to talk to the man who sat beside him, who said he was part of the militia from Massachusetts. The militias only practiced shooting, not marching, and when they fought the British, they didn't line up on an open field and shoot volleys on command. Instead, they hid behind trees or buildings, and fired whenever they saw a good target. Cuff thought their way of fighting might be the best way to beat the British. But the militias didn't stay together long. After their short term, the men would return home to plant or harvest their crops, or tend to their stock. That was why maintaining the permanent Continental Army was so important.

Now that the militias had joined the Continentals, they had to follow more rules than they were used to. But they had one choice Cuff could only dream of. They were free to go home and visit their families as they pleased. He couldn't wait for the day he'd become free to visit his family. It would be a very long visit . . . he might never leave!

The sun was setting behind dark clouds when the men finished their review. Nat came over to the tree with four of the men who had been marching with the First Rhode Island Regiment. Three of them seemed to be in their twenties; one seemed a bit older. They all had strong arms and broad shoulders and looked very impressive in their uniforms. "Cuff, these are the other men in our unit."

Cuff smiled shyly at them, "Hello."

"This is Big John, Peter, Jim, and Jack." Nat continued. "That should be easy enough for you to remember. Fellows, this is Cuff."

As they walked back to their tent, Jim, Big John, and Peter, the younger men, bombarded Cuff with questions: where he was from, who had sent him, what kind of work he did. Jack, the older man with a thick scar on his forehead, seemed more reserved.

When they got back to their tent, Jack picked up his knife and a partially carved piece of wood. Three wooden animal figurines, a quail, a deer, and a horse, lay at the foot of his bedroll.

"How does it feel to be here?" Big John, the tallest one of the group, asked.

"I wouldn't want to be anywhere else in the world," Cuff said, "except with my family." He bit his lip. The others stared at the fire, silent for a moment.

"I didn't want to join the army at first," Jack said, quietly, the head of a bear emerging from his wood. "But it sure beats working for the iron works. When I get out of here as a freeman, I'll never have to look at a hot furnace again!"

"I'm with you all the way," said Peter. He was shorter than Big John, with a gruffer voice. He, too, had worked for the iron works before joining the army.

As the sun dropped closer to the trees, the air stayed sticky with no wind to cool them. They rebuilt the cooking fire outside their tent. Cuff's stomach had been growling all afternoon and he welcomed the aroma of beef stew. "This is the last of the beef," Nat explained. "All we have left is a bit of salt pork. The local farmers have been very generous with their livestock, but we'll probably have to go foraging in the next few days."

"I could eat anything now," Cuff said, checking to see if the beef was cooked yet. "My last real meal was yesterday." Though the others were tired of stew, it tasted wonderful to Cuff!

"How long have you been in the army, Nat?" he asked.

"Four months," Nat said. "I've been in since East Greenwich training. All the men in our tent started there."

"Then you know how to shoot," Cuff assumed. "Mr. Barker showed me once, but now I'd better get good at it."

"You will," Nat said, with a grin. "They'll have us drilling every morning and afternoon while we're camped here. You'd better master the three salutes, too, right men?" He looked around at the others, who agreed. Jack had wandered away to another tent.

Nat and the other men demonstrated how and when to use each salute. Cuff picked them up easily. He sat on the ground, outside the tent, with Nat, Big John, Peter, and Jim, trying to stay cool. Cuff was beginning to feel comfortable in this new life. He had never had friends like these before. He listened as Jim talked about his life before the army. Cuff was surprised to learn that Jim was already a freeman, and his parents were free, too.

"There are about thirty free men in the First Rhode Island," Jim explained to Cuff. "But back in 1776, when the colonies broke away from England, the new Continental Congress didn't allow blacks in the army."

"But you're here now," Cuff said.

"Most definitely," said Jim. "I've got a farm up by Warren, and I sure don't want the British taxing my hard work."

"You have a farm?" Cuff asked, incredulously. "Of your very own?"

Jim chuckled. "Sure, Cuff," he said. "Just think what you have to look forward to."

Cuff was too amazed to do anything but nod.

"This is the best part of being in the First Rhode Island," said Nat, who sat across from him. "Having people to talk to . . . friends."

"I was thinking that, too," Cuff said. "In the last four years, the only other person I've talked to regularly is Susie, the Barker's cook and housemaid . . . and she's nearly fifty years old!" *Not someone to share my dreams with*, he thought.

"I've got some important news," Jack said, coming out of the darkness. "That French admiral has left, taking all his ships with him!"

"D'Estaing?" Jim asked.

"That's him," Jack said. "And word just came that the British are sending battleships and more infantrymen this way."

"Word? Who from? Was it Admiral Howe?" Cuff asked, remembering how he'd heard the British colonel tell Mr. Barker the Continental plans wouldn't mean anything once Admiral Howe arrived with reinforcements.

"That's the one," Jack said, impressed. "D'Estaing took his ships out to stop them."

"I saw the French ships sailing away just before I left Paradise Farm," Cuff said. Now he realized they'd had good reason to leave.

A humid breeze began to blow as hazy, yellow clouds moved across the sky. "A storm is coming," Big John said, standing up. Leaves rustled in the wind.

"It's going to be a bad one, too," Cuff observed. "It's coming in off the sea."

"We better hammer these tent poles a little deeper," said Jim.

As they prepared the tent for the storm, Cuff couldn't stop thinking about what he had heard. A black farmer with his own land!

That'll be me one day.

FIVE

CUFF AWOKE TO A BLAST OF COLD AIR.
The wind was howling fiercely in the darkness
outside. As he jumped from his bedroll, he realized
one side of the tent—poles and everything—had
been yanked out of the ground by the strong wind. A
thick rain beat down on them as they sloshed around
the muddy ground.

"I need some help!" Jack cried, from several feet
away. "Cuff! Give me a hand."

Cuff hurried over to help Jack push one of the
tent poles back into the ground as the other men
raced around trying to protect their muskets, uniforms, and food supplies from getting wet. Just as
Cuff and Jim pushed the tent pole back down, the
pole next to it rose.

"I'll get it!" Nat called, lunging over two disor-
derly bedrolls to reach the pole. "But there goes
another one."

Having spent his whole life on the island, Cuff
had seen many storms, but none as severe as this
one. There were so many flashes of lightning, the
men looked forward to periods of total darkness. The
thunder boomed louder than thousands of firing

muskets. Though he wouldn't admit it to anyone, Cuff longed for his cot in the barn at Paradise Farm. Though the roof often leaked, at least it was more solid than this flimsy tent.

The wind and rain pounded them all night. There was no chance for sleep since the blankets were all drenched. Finally, at dawn, calm set in. Nat and Jim worked on securing the tent poles so they wouldn't fly up again while Cuff and the others drained the puddles that had formed in their tent. Everyone searched in vain for a dry place to keep things. Most of the tents in the camp had been damaged in some way. A large tree limb had fallen on one of them, ripping a large hole in the center. Another tent had blown away. Branches and twigs littered the ground as leaves dripped from above.

Without warning, a clap of thunder and a flash of lightning shook the camp. The new storm was worse than the first. The sky grew darker; hailstones larger than musketballs hammered at the tents; rain leaked through the canvas walls. The smell of rotting cabbage around the tent grew stronger and stronger. Cuff shivered in his wet shirt, wishing he were in front of the fireplace in the Barkers' kitchen. Wind and rain didn't come through those walls.

The storm raged through the morning and past noon. The men became used to the sound of cracking, crashing tree branches, booming thunder, and pouring rain. Cuff and his tent mates took turns pushing the tent poles back into the mushy ground.

The storm lasted for two full days and three nights. There was water everywhere. Since the men couldn't build fires, they ate all the rations left in their haversacks. On the second night, Cuff sat beside Nat on the windy side of the tent, which they'd found helped keep it from blowing over. Their attempts to sleep sitting up didn't work very well. A cold, wet wind bit into their backs, but by now they were used to it. They were also used to being drenched and no longer felt awkward huddling together to stay warm.

"I've never been in a storm this bad," Nat declared, shouting above the sound of pounding rain.

"It wouldn't be so bad if I was back at Paradise Farm with sturdy walls and a roof," Cuff shouted back. Suddenly, he realized that he didn't know anything about Nat's background. Nat had been so busy telling him about the army that the subject had never come up. "Where did you live before joining the army?" Cuff asked.

"I lived in Providence," Nat yelled. "Worked in a blacksmith shop. It was awful. My mother was the house servant for the blacksmith's wife. She was nice, but my master was horrible. He whacked hot iron all day, and I was always afraid he would hit me with that giant hammer. He wasn't a very good blacksmith either, so when the war spilled into Providence, he closed the shop and became an officer. Sold me to the army right off so his wife would have money while he was gone."

"Is your mama still with the smith's wife?" Cuff asked.

Nat shrugged. "I don't know. With all this fighting,

I might never see her again."

Cuff hugged his knees close to his body. "Same here," he said, sadly. "I don't know if I'll ever see my family again."

"Were they with you at the Barkers' farm?" Nat asked. With the storm dying down, he no longer had to yell.

"No," Cuff said. "They lived on another farm that belongs to Widow Beckham. Five years ago, the Beckhams owned my whole family. But when Mr. Beckham died, his widow sold me. Last I knew, my folks, and my younger brother were all still working that farm. I guess my brother isn't so little anymore. She'll probably sell him or give him more work to do. With the war and all, it's hard to guess what's become of any of them. They were all fine the last Sunday that Mr. Barker let me visit, though."

"The blacksmith would never have given me a day off," Nat said. "You were lucky."

"I guess I was," Cuff said. "But I'd do anything to see them right now."

"I know how you feel," Nat said. "You know, we've both had three owners, counting the Rhode Island Regiment. Even though we have our freedom paper, we're not free to leave till this war is over. I don't feel one bit free, and won't, till I can choose my own life."

Cuff pulled his muddy blanket around him and began to drift off to sleep. *How can my clothes smell like sweat*, he wondered, *when for two days I've done nothing but shiver?*

*　　*　　*

The sun finally came out the next morning. Cuff groaned as he looked through his belongings. His haversack and knapsack were heavy with mud, but when he reached inside the knapsack, he was relieved to find that his freedom paper was still dry. To make sure it stayed that way, he wrapped it in a piece of oiled canvas and secured it inside his shirt. *That's where it's going to stay from now on*, he told himself.

Several men had died during the storm, and several others were coughing and sneezing. Six horses had been killed by hailstones and falling tree limbs. Cuff was glad he wasn't assigned to digging graves. But he would have rather gone foraging for food with Nat than what he was assigned to do. He and several other men spent the entire morning down at the beach making ammunition. Cuff's job was to hold lumps of lead in a big, long-handled pot over a fire. It was hot, dirty work, and he had to make several trips to the water barrel to fill his canteen. Just as the sun began to dry their clothes, sweat soaked them again. The men he worked with tied rags around their foreheads to absorb the sweat. Cuff did the same.

When the lead was melted, he had to pour the liquid into metal molds. When the molds cooled, the balls were dumped out. Men with heavy pinchers cut off the tails that had formed where the hot lead had entered the mold, making sure the balls were round. Another man collected the clipped-off tails and tossed them back in with the lead to be melted again. There were large molds for making artillery

cannon balls. The small, cherry-sized molds, were for the shot to be used in the muskets, and for the grapeshot to be used in the smaller cannons.

Since the wood was wet, the smoke was thick and dark. It was difficult to breathe, and even harder to see. Cuff tried to avoid spilling hot lead on his hands and legs, but it wasn't easy. Every once in a while he heard a pained shriek from one of the other men. Despite minor accidents, nobody was seriously burned. Around noon they took a break and headed back to their tents, leaving neat pyramids of cannon balls and bushel baskets filled with ammunition for the muskets on the beach.

Cuff couldn't believe that it was only noon. He was tired and eager for the day to end. Just as he reached the tent, an officer approached him.

"Where's that new man, Cuff Barker?" the officer asked.

"That's me, sir," Cuff answered quickly, standing as straight as he could.

"Very well, Private. You've been assigned to Major Samuel Ward. You'll deliver messages and do chores for him . . . anything he asks. Do you understand, Private?"

"Yes, sir!" Cuff exclaimed, hoping he gave the correct salute.

"Eat quickly and report in twenty minutes," the officer ordered. When the man walked away, Cuff noticed his hands were trembling.

"Cuff, are you all right?" Cuff turned to find Nat and Jim, who had just come up with the food they had foraged this morning.

"I've been assigned to work for Major Ward," he said hesitantly.

"Impressive!" Jim said, patting Cuff on the back.

Cuff suddenly felt dizzy. "I need to hurry." The idea of working for one of the officers in charge of the entire regiment made him nervous. What if he made mistakes? What if he didn't work fast enough? What if he didn't wake up on time? What if they sent him back to Paradise Farm?

"You have nothing to worry about," Nat said, as if he had heard Cuff's thoughts. "I was nervous before I worked for Major Talbot. I didn't know anything about building boats. But it turned out to be easy. Whatever I didn't know, someone else showed me. You'll be fine."

*   *   *

As it turned out, Nat was right. Cuff enjoyed his first day of working for Major Ward, a tall man whose blue eyes twinkled when he smiled. Though it was only the first day, he taught Cuff everything he'd need to know and encouraged him to ask questions if he didn't understand something. By the end of the afternoon, Cuff had learned how to set up the major's desk and prepare it for him to write letters. He had also memorized all the names and descriptions of officers that he'd be delivering messages to and from. In addition to the more important jobs, he learned to set up the major's small camp stove.

Other aides explained how to set up the big white tent that was shaped like a box. Cuff already knew how to scour pots. At the end of the day, a man came to Major Ward with news that ten British deserters had surrendered to the Continental Army. "The deserters said the French ships destroyed two fortifications in Newport when they chased the British out of the harbor," he reported. "And the British got pounded harder than we did with this storm, being out on the water. Word is that we'll march on Newport tomorrow."

*   *   *

It was nearly dark before Cuff headed back to his tent. All around him fires burned low, and men on blankets were scattered about. Though the sun had been hot today, the blankets were still damp and the insides of the tents were musty. They would sleep under the stars tonight.

"Good to see you, Cuff!" Nat called out from beside their fire. I saved you some dinner. Cuff gratefully accepted the trencher of salt pork and watercress. "How was your day?"

"Great," Cuff said, grinning.

"That's really something," Peter said. "You getting called to help Major Ward."

"I guess," Cuff said. "I just hope I do a good job. Some of the names are confusing, like there's a General Nathanael Greene and a Colonel Christopher Greene, who is above Major Ward in command of our regiment. But I could tell Major Ward expected me to know that General Varnum is the brigade commander in charge of our regiment and several other battalions."

"Varnum's a good man," Jack said, moving closer to the others. He had just finished carving a rabbit out of a tree limb. "He's the one who finally got General Washington to approve of black men fighting in the Army."

"He's the one who set up this regiment," said Jim.

"And gave us our chance for freedom," Nat pitched in.

"Lots of white folks still don't like the idea," Peter agreed. "Remember when we were marching from East Greenwich to Providence?" The others nodded. "White folks came to stare at us in every town along the way."

"Some people said we couldn't be trusted with weapons," Nat said, bitterly. "They said we'd run off instead of fight."

"Oh, we'll fight all right," Jim said, raising his fist.

"We've got a lot to fight for," Cuff added, lying back to look at the starry sky. "We have to help win this war if we want to be free."

SIX

BEFORE DAWN ON HIS FIFTH DAY IN THE army, Cuff woke to the sound of drums beating the signal for the soldiers to strike their tents and prepare to march. It had been announced the night before that they'd be advancing to Newport.

Cuff had never heard so many different noises as the men rolled up their blankets and tents: men grunting under heavy loads, officers giving orders, horses whinnying, muskets clanking together, and men talking and joking with one another. Before setting off, each soldier was issued a loaf of bread to last him until that evening.

Cuff wolfed down a chunk of bread, and hurriedly helped strike Major Ward's tent. An hour later, the drumbeat changed, signaling the soldiers to form ranks. Like everyone else, Cuff pulled on his knapsack, blanket tied securely in the top straps, and slung his wooden canteen and haversack over his left shoulder. Instead of walking with the other soldiers, he had to march beside Major Ward, who rode his horse.

Two cannon shots were fired, signaling the men to form columns. Then three cannon shots were fired, and the front line advanced down the hill in four columns. Cuff glanced around him, ears still ringing from the blast, as they moved forward, thrilled to be among so many officers in uniform. The gold braids, stars, and buttons on their uniforms glittered in the rising sun. *If only Nat could march by Major Ward too*, he thought, missing the companionship of his unit. He wondered if Jack had taken all his wooden animals with him.

Artillery and ammunition wagons advanced behind the front line, wheels groaning over the rocky terrain. Every few minutes a driver would curse when his wheels sunk in mud. Behind the wagons, a second line, including Nat and his other tent-mates, followed in two columns.

Damage from the devastating storm was everywhere. Uprooted trees and limbs littered meadows, corn stalks lay in deep puddles amid fields.

As much as Cuff wanted to look at the countryside around him, he was forced to watch his step. It was easy to trip on rocks and sticks in the road. At a crossroad in the next valley, the troops divided. Half the brigades continued south on East Road, while the other half—including the militia, Cuff, Major Ward, and the rest of the First Rhode Island Regiment—turned west on a smaller road, which led to West Road on the other side of the hill.

Shady trees provided some relief from the increasing heat, but that didn't stop the militiamen from grumbling. Cuff knew no one in his regiment, however, would be grumbling. They were used to long days, heavy burdens, and hard work. Just thinking about it made him stand a little straighter and pick up his pace. He was proud to be part of the First Rhode Island Regiment!

Cuff caught a glimpse of Narragansett Bay sparkling far below the rocky hills. Soon they started down toward bay level, passing meadows with yellow and white flowers along the way. Cuff looked up briefly and caught a glimpse of a yellow bird with black wings; it sang as it flew.

Shortly after noon, as they marched along a set of easy, rolling slopes, Cuff recognized the high, rocky hill to their left. It was Barker's Hill, his home until nine days earlier. To Cuff, it seemed like ages! He hoped Susie and the Barkers were all right, regardless of what side Mr. Barker was on.

Suddenly it dawned on him that Major Ward might not know that enemy troops were living on the Barker farm. He wondered if he should tell him. He'd be betraying Mr. Barker if he did. But didn't he owe it to the Continental Army? He bit his lip. If he didn't say anything, all their confidential plans could be ruined. Even if Major Ward scolded him for failing to provide the information sooner, he had to speak up.

"Major Ward!" he blurted out loudly. His face grew hot as several men turned to stare at him. "Major Ward, sir!" he said again, this time louder.

"What is it, Private?" the major asked, looking down from his horse.

"That's Barker's Hill over there," Cuff said, in a higher voice than usual. "And anybody on the top of that hill with a spy glass could see everything we're

doing."

Major Ward looked toward the top of the hill and then back to Cuff. "Yes, I suppose they could," he said.

"Sir," Cuff said more confidently, "The British . . . they're on Barker's Hill at Paradise Farm." Major Ward, and all the officers in hearing distance, stared at Cuff as he continued to speak. "A British colonel moved into the Barker house and his troops are camped nearby." Cuff swallowed hard. "I . . . uh . . . guess I should have said something sooner."

"Don't worry, Private," Major Ward said, smiling. "We've gotten word that the British are gone from there. They moved close to Newport after the storm. Our advance is no secret anyway."

By mid-afternoon, they came to a stop, only a short distance away from Newport. Cuff shuddered at the memory of Newport in flames. He imagined that the Beckham farm was in ruins by now, and, again, he hoped his family was safe.

As orders were relayed along the line, the troops began fanning off to Cuff's left. In the distance he could see the troops they'd separated from on East Road, now spewing toward them. Soon the Continental Army stretched across nearly the whole island. All along this line, artillery was aimed directly at the outer defenses of Newport.

"The British will never be able to escape our blockade," said a nearby officer.

Cuff agreed silently, as the drummers signaled them to march on. He looked back toward Barker's Hill and wondered what Susie was doing now. Had she taken over his garden work? Was Mrs. Barker helping her? He wished he could have told them a few things about the different plants. He wondered when Mr. Barker's next hunting trip was. The thought of Mr. Barker made him wonder, once again, which side he was on. He had an awful feeling that he already knew.

From the direction of Newport, a cannonball streaked toward them and, before Cuff had time to blink, smacked short into a narrow stream. Other cannon exploded in the distance. With his heart thudding, Cuff suddenly became aware of how serious the situation was. He was no longer "Mr. Barker's boy." Now he was a soldier on his way to do battle with the British. The realization caused his hands to tremble.

Another cannonball streaked toward them, this one also fell short. It bounced, and then rolled toward them but nothing happened.

"The British are just letting us know they've seen us," Major Ward muttered. "It's nothing to worry about. The firing is coming from the small fort at Green End—not Newport, where the majority of them are." The drummers began a new rhythm, the signal to set up camp. Cuff and two aides helped set up Major Ward's tent and writing desk. As the major dipped his quill in ink and began to write, Cuff made up the major's cot and hung up his uniforms. He tried to be as quiet as possible.

"Private," Major called, sifting sand across the paper to dry the ink, then folding it and sealing it with candle wax. "Take this to General Sullivan."

"Yes, sir!" Cuff saluted and then hurried off to General Sullivan's quarters, a few hundred yards away on Honeyman Hill. He spent the rest of the afternoon shuttling back and forth, delivering messages from one commander to the next. It was a good way to get to know the layout of the new camp, which curved far to the southeast toward Paradise Farm, and west toward the water.

Late in the afternoon, when he returned from delivering a second message from General Sullivan, Major Ward looked troubled.

"Is there anything more, sir?" Cuff asked, wondering if he'd done something wrong.

"I need more help around here," Major Ward replied, running his fingers through his brown hair wearily. "You can't possibly deliver all the messages I write soon enough."

Cuff stared at the ground and bit his lip.

"You're doing fine, Cuff," the major reassured. "There's just too much work for one person."

Cuff straightened and smiled. "What about Nat Potter?" he suggested. "He's a good, hard worker, and smart, too."

"Very well," Major Ward said. "Bring him here tomorrow morning."

"Yes, sir!" Cuff said, smiling. He worked for another two hours and then set off in search of Nat.

By the time he found their tent, cook fires were already blazing. The smell of onions, mutton, and steaming cabbage reminded Cuff how hungry he was. He hadn't eaten since breakfast.

"Where's Nat?" Cuff asked, dropping his knapsack, canteen, and haversack. Jack put down a wooden owl he'd been carving. "Night duty again."

*   *   *

The next morning, Cuff began to worry. He knew Nat would be tired from night duty, but he didn't want Major Ward to be angry at him for not returning with another messenger. He hoped Nat turned up soon.

Just as he was about to leave for Major Ward's tent, Nat showed up. His hair, shirt, and overalls were covered with dirt. Sighing with relief, Cuff thought about making a joke but then changed his mind. Nat looked too exhausted for humor. He also looked too exhausted to spend the day delivering messages.

"Where've you been?" Cuff asked. "I've got good news."

"I spent most of the night helping to dig a ditch for a new protective barrier," Nat mumbled. "Going to have to dig again tonight, too. My arms feel like they want to fall off. My back aches like I'm an old man. I'm off until dark and heading straight for some sleep. Wish I'd been chosen for your job, Cuff. You sure were lucky."

"Guess what," Cuff said, smiling. Nat looked at him in a daze. "You're lucky too. Major Ward needs another messenger and I volunteered you."

"Are you pulling my leg?" Nat asked, now more alert.

"I'm completely serious," Cuff said. "But you have to get washed up and changed. We have to report to him in twenty minutes."

"I feel better already," Nat said. He hurried and was ready in twelve minutes. They walked toward Major Ward's tent together.

"It was some march, yesterday," Cuff said, "I . . ." he stopped at the sound of a thud in the stream to the south of them.

"Good thing their aim is poor," Nat said, quickening his pace toward the tent. A cannon boomed from their own lines, followed by another, and then another. One was so close that it shook the earth.

"I sure hope the French show up soon," Cuff said, hoping his voice didn't reveal the panic he felt.

SEVEN

BOTH BRITISH AND AMERICAN CANNONS continued to roar, one after another. It was rare that an hour passed without at least one explosion.

Major Ward was very happy with Nat and praised Cuff for his excellent choice. The two privates spent the next few days running messages from one officer's tent to another. They hurried up hills and down hills, under shade and sun, through rain and fog, across meadows and briar patches, avoiding rocks that could make them stumble. The messages were urgent, leaving no time to admire the view or observe yellow birds with black wings that sang when they flew. They knew to watch out for the artillery wagons and be ready to clamp their hands over their ears if they saw the big torch being put to the cannon fuse. The noise of firing cannon left their ears ringing a long time afterward.

One morning, it was so foggy, Cuff could barely see. By afternoon, the fog was so bad that Major Ward dismissed Cuff and Nat for the rest of the day. "I believe there's an earthwork that needs to be built," he said.

The two boys worked for the rest of the afternoon, helping to make an embankment in the earth for protection. Jack stood in the trench, filling a bucket with dirt. When the bucket was full, another man lifted up the bucket to Cuff. Cuff emptied it onto the growing dirt pile, which was slowly rising to become a wall.

By four o' clock, the fog began to lift, and cannon fire came more frequently from both sides. As he worked, ears ringing, Cuff counted seventeen shots in a row! He nearly forgot what silence was like. He also forgot what it felt like not to have mud clinging to part of his body.

A cannonball shot by the British landed about fifteen feet away, shaking the earth and making Cuff's heart pound. "When do you think we're going to fight?" Cuff asked Nat.

"I sure wouldn't want to fight in this fog," Nat said.

"I can't imagine why the British would either," said another man. "No navy can sail in this."

"First that storm, and now this," Jack said, shaking his head. Cuff looked up and froze. A cannonball streaked through the fog and crashed amid some bushes only ten feet away. It bounced high, smashed a rock to pieces, and came straight for them.

"Get back!" Cuff yelled, shoving Nat away from the bucket and diving toward the ground.

The cannonball thudded into the bucket that had just been filled with dirt, then crashed into the dirt wall.

Cuff scrambled up and peered into the trench, surprised to see Nat looking back at him, trembling. "You all right?" Cuff asked. "I didn't mean to push you into the trench."

"That was close!" Nat exclaimed, with wide eyes. "We could have been killed."

Jack was looking down, his face drawn. The iron cannonball, as big as a pumpkin, had landed only two inches from his foot. "Sometimes I wonder if it's worth it," he muttered, edging away from the cannonball.

"There goes all our hard work," Nat said, still trembling. He looked up at the smashed wall and climbed out of the trench.

"Private Barker! Private Potter!"

It was Major Ward's aide, the flaps of his coat bright against the uprooted earth. Cuff and Nat clambered into the trench and then up the other side. "Yes, sir!" They saluted together.

"You're both to report to the major, at once," the aide said.

Cuff and Nat saluted the man again and took off at a run, relieved to be away from the front lines. "You saved my life, Cuff," Nat said. "I don't know how I'll ever thank you."

Cuff shrugged. "You'd have done the same for me and you know it."

When they arrived at the large white, squared-off tent, Major Ward was in good spirits. "French ships have returned to the bay," he said, handing them three letters each. "We have to spread the word immediately."

*　　　*　　　*

As Cuff raced around delivering the good news,

everyone seemed to be in high spirits. Now that the French ships had returned to the bay, they were sure they would win Newport back very soon.

But two days later when Cuff and Nat arrived at Major Ward's tent, the major was livid. "D'Estaing is saying he can't stay. I need someone to contact General Lafayette immediately." The Marquis de Lafayette was a French nobleman who had come to America the previous year to fight alongside the Americans. Major Ward turned to Cuff, "You'll have to go by horseback." He jotted a quick note. "Give my aides this, and tell them I said to saddle a horse for you. This is extremely urgent."

Cuff couldn't believe it. He was going to ride a horse through this camp full of white men? Was he really going to meet the distinguished General Lafayette? He took the note to the aide outside. The aide's eyebrows rose, but he ran off and returned ten minutes later with a saddled horse. Another aide helped Cuff mount. Cuff looked down from the back of the high horse. Everything looked different from up here. He cautiously gave the horse a kick and headed down the road.

At first he bounced along like a sack of potatoes in the saddle, but soon he grew used to the rhythm of the cantering horse beneath him. It was nicer than walking or riding in a wagon. *Maybe someday*, he thought, *I can have a horse of my own.* He passed much of the same landscape he had seen on the march to Newport, but this time the trip was much quicker. It took him about an hour and a half to reach the estate of Metcalf Bowler, a little south of Butts Hill, where General Lafayette was staying.

Cuff had passed the estate when he'd journeyed from Paradise Farm, but it had been hidden in the darkness. Still, he wondered how he could have missed such a large, impressive house. As he tied the horse to a post, he admired the ornate carvings on the front of the house. He walked down a flagstone path to a side door that was slightly ajar. He knocked and the door was answered by a dark skinned man, rubbing dirt from his hands.

"I'm looking—" Cuff began and then glanced past the man, and gasped with amazement. There, in front of him, was a garden room enclosed by glass walls. The garden was filled with plants and trees Cuff had never seen before. He gazed with awe at a tree with leaves as long as his legs.

"This garden!" Cuff exclaimed, forgetting for a moment why he was there. "It's—"

"It's a greenhouse, lad," the man said. "I take it the plants interest you."

"Oh, yes!" Cuff said, enthusiastically. "I like to grow things and work the land myself. When I'm free, I'm going to have my own farm, and—" Cuff blushed with embarrassment. He was a soldier—a soldier on an urgent mission. "I—I'm sorry. I'm looking for the Marquis de Lafayette. I've got an important message for him."

The gardener chuckled. "He's staying in the summerhouse at the end of this lane. There are plenty of gardens there, too. Go have a look."

"Thank you," Cuff said, beginning to salute by habit. Then he scurried back along the flagstone path.

"Good luck with your plans for freedom," the man called after him.

"Thank you, sir."

Cuff found the French nobleman at a smaller, yet beautiful, house surrounded by exquisite gardens and marble statues. The Marquis de Lafayette, a slightly built man with curled hair, came to the door himself. He was much younger than Cuff expected—not yet twenty-one—and splendidly dressed. He wore a white shirt covered by a gold vest with a red sash below it, gold pants, a blue jacket with broad gold bands, and shiny, black boots. "Come in, come in," Lafayette said, in a friendly manner. Cuff stood in the main hall, admiring the shiny marble floors and the large oil paintings on the walls. As the marquis read Major Ward's letter, his forehead furrowed.

"Please, sit while I get ready. I'm coming back with you as far as General Sullivan's headquarters."

"Sir, may I wait outside?" Cuff suggested, hoping he wasn't being too demanding.

"Yes, lad," the marquis said. "Go ahead. But get your horse ready."

Cuff brought the horse to the summer house. As he strolled through the gardens, he recognized many vegetables, herbs, and flowers, which he used to grow for Mrs. Barker. "Working in the garden gives you a clear head," his father used to say. Cuff missed his father. *My father would be impressed with the marquis' garden, that was for sure*, he thought.

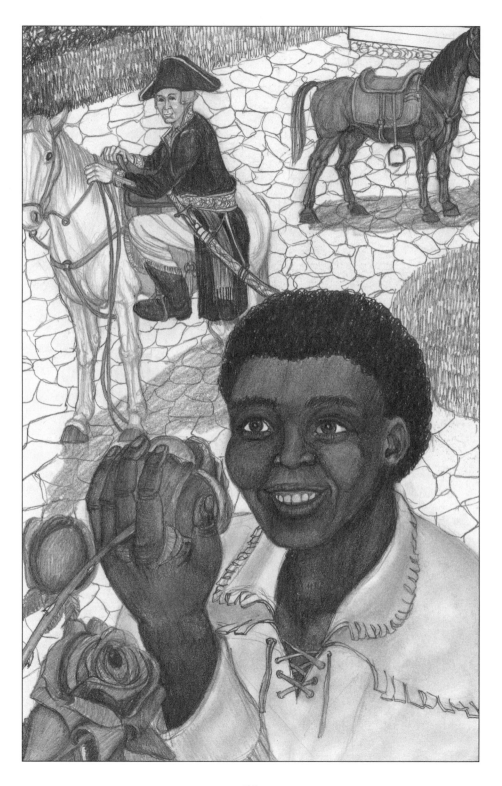

Plants spread out in neat patterns. His favorites were the sections filled with red and yellow flowers. Cuff bent to smell a red rose and wished he could stay there forever.

"Lad!" the marquis called. He had a knapsack slung over one shoulder and was leading his horse. Cuff hurried over and climbed awkwardly onto his mount. He couldn't believe he was going to ride back to the camp with the Marquis de Lafayette! As the horses galloped, the marquis asked about Cuff's family and his hopes for freedom. *He's really interested!* Cuff thought wonderingly. After a while, they both rode in silence. Cuff knew that there was a lot on the general's mind. When Lafayette turned off to General Sullivan's headquarters he returned Cuff's salute. Cuff was speechless. Never before had a white man given him so much respect.

Later that afternoon, when he saw his tentmates, oiling and cleaning their muskets outside the tent, they wanted to hear all about it. "Can you believe that!" laughed Peter. "Old Cuff here riding horses with the Marquis de Lafayette." The others laughed happily.

"From what I could make of it," said Cuff, "we might not be able to count on the French Navy to help us fight for Newport. The storm tore them up pretty bad. The admiral's flagship is in tow, its main mast gone! D'Estaing wants to go back to Boston for repairs. General Lafayette rowed out to the ships to speak with him."

"That storm hit the British hard, too," Big John

said. "I heard we lost track of the British fleet. They're nowhere in sight."

"When I delivered a message to General Varnum today, he said that they've gone back to New York for repairs," Nat offered.

"I wonder how he found that out," Cuff said.

"A spy, most likely," Nat answered. "Someone behind the British lines must be getting information to us."

"I'd like to shake that fellow's hand," Peter said.

"I get the feeling that some people just *say* they're Tories," Jim said, as he oiled the underside of his musket, "especially those living on this island. They pretend to side with the British so they won't have to worry about their property being taken, or worse, being thrown in jail."

Cuff stared at Jim thoughtfully. Peter looked over at Nat, who had finished cleaning his musket.

"You'd better make certain your long piece is in good working order, Nat. And you, Marquis de Cuff. Has anyone shown you how to fire a musket, yet?"

Cuff shrugged. "Mr. Barker showed me a few times, but that's about it."

"Here," Peter said, handing Cuff his rifle. It was nearly as long as Cuff was tall, barrel heavy at the end of the wooden stock. "Let's see you load."

Cuff took a deep breath, hoping he remembered the sequence correctly. He hoisted the weapon to the crook of his left arm, lifted the firelock halfway up, and opened the pan. Then Peter handed him a paper cartridge.

"Just go through the motions, Cuff," Big John said. "We don't want to fire a gun here in camp."

Cuff laughed nervously and concentrated on the cartridge. "I bite off the top of the paper, and cover the open space with my thumb so I won't spill back powder or lose the ball," he began. "Then I shake a little of the powder into the flash pan." He pretended to put powder in the small round pan that stuck out behind the firelock. "Then I close the pan, pour the rest of the powder into the barrel, and drop the paper and ball in the barrel, too." He tilted back the musket and pulled the brass rod loose from the hooks under the barrel. "Then I shove the ball and paper tight onto the powder." He pushed the rod into the barrel and then returned the ramrod to its proper place. "There, it's ready to fire," he said, looking up at last.

"Good work," Peter said. "Now practice that over and over. You need to be able to do it real fast."

"Good shooters do it so fast, they can get off three or four shots a minute," Jim said.

"But I don't have a musket," Cuff said, handing it back to Peter.

"True," said Peter. "But come a battle, you might need to load for someone else."

"Why don't you practice on mine, Cuff?" Nat volunteered. "We can share for now."

Cuff nodded with gratitude, but inside he felt queasy. He understood what Peter had meant. He might have to load a musket for a wounded soldier who couldn't load for himself. As much as he wanted the war to be over, he didn't like to think about the consequences. Fighting in a war meant people would get hurt. Some would die. If it were a stranger, it would be bad enough—but what if it were Nat or one of his other tent mates? What if it were himself? What if he never lived to become a free man?

EIGHT

THE NEXT MORNING WHEN CUFF AND NAT arrived at Major Ward's tent, the officer announced wearily that the French had decided to go back to Boston after all. Cuff's heart sank; he knew that there was little chance of winning a battle without the big guns of the French Navy to help rout the British.

The removal of the French placed the regiment in conflict. Some soldiers wanted to attack right away, before the British received naval support. Others thought the whole campaign was wasted. Over the next few days, Cuff noticed there were more and more empty spaces where tents had once stood.

One afternoon, Cuff watched a father and son from the Rhode Island militia packing up their belongings. The son was kicking rocks into a fire pit.

"Won't you need that fire later?" Cuff asked, curiously.

"No indeed," the son replied. "We're going home."

"But we haven't taken Newport yet!" Cuff exclaimed.

"Probably won't, either, without the French

fleet," said the father. "Maybe you men in the First Rhode Island don't have a choice, but we do. We only signed on for twenty days. We've got crops in Tiverton to tend and families to care for."

I have a family, too, Cuff thought to himself angrily, watching the two men walk away.

As more and more men left, the sound of cannon fire off in the distance grew louder and louder. "It seems so unfair," Cuff said to Nat, as he loaded his trencher with cod and watercress. "I wish I could come and go as I please."

"I know what you mean," Nat said as he waited for his meal to cool. "How can we force the British off the island if our own troops are leaving? Almost all of the volunteers have gone home."

"I wish I could say the same for myself," Big John exclaimed. "I have a sweetheart waiting for me at home, and if we stay here much longer, I doubt she'll even recognize me."

"At least you have a sweetheart," Jim said. "All I've got is my mother, and I have no idea what farm she's working on."

"If half of the forces are gone, then why are there so many tents?" Peter asked.

"To fool the British," said Cuff. "I hope it works as well on them as it did on you." Peter grinned.

"It doesn't look good," said Jack, whittling a mouse's ear. "The British control Newport, New York, and Staten Island. If we had stopped them here, the French could have gone right down the coast and forced them out of the other ports. The war could've been over by now."

"We must keep our spirits up," Jim said. "There are still quite a few Continental regiments."

But the next afternoon, Cuff and Nat heard more bad news from Major Ward. "The British fleet is back on the sea," the major said, over the sound of cannon fire.

"Now, Cuff, I'd like you to prepare my writing materials," Major Ward continued. "And Nat, I'd like you to start fires in every fire pit you see so British spies don't see anything out of the ordinary. The last thing we need is for them to mount an attack because they know we're outnumbered."

While Cuff set up the paper, ink, and quill, a message came from General Sullivan's new headquarters, west of his former location on Honeyman Hill. "The Marquis de Lafayette is on his way to Boston," Major Ward read out loud. "He's planning to try to convince the admiral to sail his fleet back here right away. If he does, we still might have a chance."

"That's good news, sir," Cuff said, honored that the major was confiding in him.

"I hope so," said Major Ward. "The marquis has promised to bring us word personally."

Cuff remembered how nice the marquis had been to him and hoped to meet him again some day. He'd love to spend more time in that garden.

The major continued to read. "A recent message confirms that the British have abandoned all but one of their outer earthworks." Cuff wondered if the message had come from the same spy who'd reported that the

British had returned to New York for repairs.

"So all of the British are behind their main defenses on the outskirts of Newport," Cuff said, hesitantly.

"Exactly," Major Ward said, looking pleased.

"Then we should have time to attack before Admiral Howe arrives with the British fleet, sir," Cuff said, wondering where he'd gotten the nerve to speak up like that.

"Hopefully," said Major Ward, "the departure of the militiamen has really weakened us. We have about fifty-four hundred men remaining at this camp and on Butts Hill. That's a very low number. We'll just have to hope the British reinforcements don't arrive before Lafayette does."

That evening a meeting was held outside Major Ward's tent. When Cuff arrived with his unit, he noticed the Major's sad and worried expression in the firelight. As the men gathered around in the darkness, the major began to speak.

"We've been on the island for almost twenty days, and I know things haven't gone as you'd expected," he began. "Our food supply is low, and it's up to you to find any food you can. But please try to make all your actions seem normal. I'm certain British spyglasses are on us. We'll keep the fires going past dark and leave wood nearby so the rear guard can keep them burning. After that . . . " The major tried to smile as everyone waited for him to finish. "After that," he continued, "we'll have to retreat to Butts Hill. And there will be no drumming this time."

No one said a word, but Cuff could feel the defeat in the air. The men went back to their tents, packed their belongings, and fed their fires in silence. Soon after, the last four brigades headed back along West Road in the moonlight, leaving behind only guards to keep watch and maintain the fires. By the time they passed through Lawton Valley, the guards, too, had pulled out and headed north. By midnight, they had reached Turkey Hill, where their march ended. Blankets were spread on the grass as Cuff and Nat, and the other aides, set up the officers' tents. As soon as Cuff lay down on his blanket, he fell into a much needed sleep. All was quiet in the new Continental Army camp just as it was in Newport where the British slept.

NINE

IT WAS STILL DARK WHEN THE QUICK pounding of horse hooves awakened Cuff. He hadn't been up more than five minutes when Major Ward called him. "The British have started pursuit," Major Ward said. "Cuff, go down the line, and give this message to Colonel Greene."

"Yes, sir!" Cuff saluted. The urgent news made his heart race. When he returned within the hour, he found the First Rhode Island up and assembled, waiting for orders.

"At ease, men," the major said, solemnly. "One of our brigades is on Turkey Hill," he began. "We'll be aiding some other regiments in defending the right flank." He pointed, sweeping his hands over the area they'd be covering—from the slope they stood on, to a hilltop in the distance, and down to the shore. "I realize that for most of you, this will be your first real battle," he said. "Just keep in mind what we're fighting for. It is time to end British oppression and begin our freedom."

Nat and Cuff exchanged looks, knowing the freedom sought by the First Rhode Island was even more meaningful than that mentioned by the major.

The sky was just beginning to lighten when Major Ward delivered his orders.

Some men were assigned to build earthworks, while others were to reinforce an existing one near the shore. Cuff, Nat, and the rest of the First Rhode Island were assigned to forage for food. They set off immediately, each man carrying a large, empty sack.

It wasn't long before they came to a rock wall. When they climbed over it, they found themselves in a large garden filled with rows of corn stalks. Most of the stalks had been damaged by the weather. Some had been crushed by falling branches.

"No one's been here for a few weeks," Cuff observed. "See all these weeds and broken branches. A good farmer would have cleared—" he stopped suddenly and listened. "Did you hear that? It sounded like musket fire."

"We're always hearing gunfire and nothing has really happened yet," Jim said, skeptically.

"You never know," Nat whispered. "Let's stay quiet and low to the ground."

"Good idea," said Jack, dropping to his hands and knees.

"Hopefully, the walls will hide us," Big John said, creeping behind him.

Frowning, Cuff began collecting undamaged ears of corn. After adding corn to their sacks, they headed back along a stream, keeping low to the ground.

Before long, they were crawling through another abandoned vegetable garden—this one had carrots and beans. Before filling their sacks, the men picked carrots for themselves, washed them in the stream and ate them greedily.

"Do you really think we have to stay low?" Big John asked. "I haven't heard any more musket fire."

"What's that?" Jack hissed, motioning for the others to be quiet.

Listening closely, they heard a sound in the bushes on the other side of the garden.

"You all stay here," Nat said. "I'll check it out."

A few minutes later, Nat crawled back. "They're eating carrots, just like us," he whispered.

"Were they British?" Cuff asked nervously.

"No," Nat answered. "The two men I saw were wearing blue jackets with yellow trim. They seemed to be hiding from someone or something."

"They're Hessians," Jim said.

"That means trouble," Cuff said, remembering the Hessians on Mr. Barker's farm. "They get paid by the British to fight against the Americans."

When they reached camp, Cuff and Nat raced over to Major Ward's tent and told him about the Hessians.

"They're probably just deserters," one of the major's aides said.

"But they had to have something to desert from," Cuff said.

"Barker's right," Major Ward said in a serious tone. "Though the two Hessians are probably harmless, the troops they deserted from are not. They could be near." As if on cue, the crack of gunfire echoed across the camp. The major gave battle orders.

Cuff, Nat, and the rest of the First Rhode Island were assigned to one of the earthworks on a small hill near Narragansett Bay. As they lowered themselves into the trench, Cuff realized that he was the only one without a musket. All he had was his tomahawk. Though he had no desire to shoot a musket, he wanted to be able to protect himself. He bit his lip.

"Don't worry, Cuff," Nat said quietly, as if he could hear his friend's thoughts. "If you need my musket, it's here for you."

"Thanks, Nat." Cuff took a deep breath, wishing he were somewhere else.

The sound of cannon fire ripped through his thoughts. It came from the direction of Quaker Hill, to the east. Cuff remembered hunting with Mr. Barker on that very same mountain. Seconds later, more cannon fire sounded—this time from Turkey Hill—and it didn't stop.

Within minutes, cannons from Butt's Hill fired in the direction of Turkey Hill.

"I thought the Americans were on Turkey Hill!" Cuff said with alarm. His stomach felt queasy.

"Not any more," Jack said. "They've been ordered to fall back."

One of Major Ward's aides came to fetch Cuff and Nat. When they reached the major's tent, they gasped with horror at what they saw. Hundreds of American soldiers were straggling into the camp. Several were seriously wounded.

Cuff winced and looked away.

Nat put his hand on Cuff's shoulder. "Never stop

thinking of your life as a free man," he said. Cuff met his eyes. He understood.

"We thought we got them," a man with a bloody arm reported faintly. "We were hiding behind a stone wall and caught those Hessians by surprise. But there were too many of them." He flopped down onto the grass, exhausted.

A messenger galloped in from General Varnum's headquarters, sending dust in all directions. "They've taken Quaker Hill," he reported to Major Ward. "Luckily one of us saw the Hessians coming and warned everyone."

"We have to hold this flank, or the British will overrun Butts Hill!" the major declared. For the first time, Cuff detected panic in the major's voice. He didn't like it one bit.

"They have the advantage," the rider said breathlessly. "The British are now on Turkey Hill and Quaker Hill—and both hills are higher than Butts."

"All men, to arms!" the major ordered.

Before noon, the first of the fighting began. As much as he thought he was prepared, Cuff felt shocked to see his unit shooting at the enemy. He was silently grateful this time that he didn't have a musket.

Since he couldn't fight, he brought fresh ammunition and water to his comrades. He also relayed messages from Major Ward to different officers. His ears rang constantly as outgoing cannon fire shook the ground, and incoming cannonballs crashed around them.

Every few minutes a horse would squeal and fall. But the worst sounds of all were the painful shrieks and cries of men in the meadow below, where hand-to-hand combat had broken out. Soldiers stabbed out with bayonets, and beat each other with musket butts.

Cuff was too shocked to turn away from the sight of men lying on blood-stained grass or rocks. Some groaned and screamed for help. Others couldn't. Cuff was grateful when the smoke became so thick he couldn't see, even though it burned his eyes and nose.

As Cuff, staying low to the ground, hurried toward the earthworks with ammunition, he spied a group of Hessians advancing on the First Rhode Island. They loaded, fired, and reloaded their muskets in a tense, but well-rehearsed, routine. By the time he reached the earthworks to warn his unit, they were already firing back. With gunfire cracking around him, Cuff scurried back and forth, heart racing. He couldn't bear to stay with his regiment too long for fear he'd see one of them fall from enemy fire.

New cannon fire came from the bay, near the earthworks. "British ships!" a voice called.

Cuff froze behind a tree, peering out at three British ships that moved up the bay. Nat and the rest of the First Rhode Island were the closest Americans to the bay. His heart sunk as three cannonballs, one after another, landed only a few feet away from the earthwork.

Where's the French Navy when we need them? Cuff thought to himself, wiping the sweat away from his eyes with muddy hands. A cannonball landed in a bush only a few feet away from him, and the shock of the discharge knocked him to the ground. Numb to the pain, he scrambled up and ran to get more ammunition for his fellow troops.

The fighting continued through the afternoon. As the Americans shot cannonballs at the British ships, the British navy backed away. Those soldiers who could still stand were now fully engaged in the battle. One of General Varnum's other battalions held the middle near the road.

The Hessians attacked the First Rhode Island's earthwork four times, each time with fierce determination. Cuff watched proudly as the black soldiers stood their ground. They were strong, proud, and determined to win their freedom.

After firing constantly for two hours, the Hessians retreated. Cuff watched as Nat and the other men from his unit scrambled out of the trench and over the wall of the earthwork shouting fiercely and firing at the enemy. They had stopped the Hessian advance.

A little later when Cuff found Nat, Big John, Peter, Jim, and Jack exhausted but unharmed, a great sense of relief flooded over him. Without thinking, he threw his arms around Nat. "I'm so glad you're safe," he cried. Nat nodded breathlessly.

Though cannonballs continued to fly in different directions, one of Major Ward's aides instructed the First Rhode Island to care for the wounded in the valley.

"I don't know if I can do this," Cuff said to Nat as he filled a large canteen with water. He tied an extra cup to his belt. "War and shooting is hard enough, but checking to see if a man is dead or alive . . . " His voice trailed off.

"I told you," Nat said, "keep your mind focused on your life as a free man. That's the only thing that's keeping me going."

"Same here," Big John said. "Every time my finger pulls the trigger, my mind is thinking about my sweetheart at home."

In the valley, they were stunned by the number of bodies lying in pools of blood. One man had a bloody hole in the center of his chest. Another was missing an arm.

"Listen for the ones making noise," Jack said. "Those are the ones we have to help. It doesn't matter if they're American or British. The British will become prisoners of war."

The first man Cuff approached, an American with a bloody stump where his hand should be, was crying for water. Trying his best not to vomit, Cuff poured water into the man's mouth. The man started choking and coughing for air. *I've made him worse*, Cuff panicked. But when the coughing stopped, the man begged for more water. Finally, Big John helped Cuff lead the man to a cart, which would eventually bring him back to his camp.

Cuff tried to take Nat's advice, focusing on his life after the war as a free man, but he couldn't. Instead, his mind kept wandering to the men he was helping. What kind of life could a man lead without a leg? Would a man with a hole in his throat ever be able to talk again? What if *he* were the one injured? Would he want his family to see him that way?

The more men he helped, the more resourceful

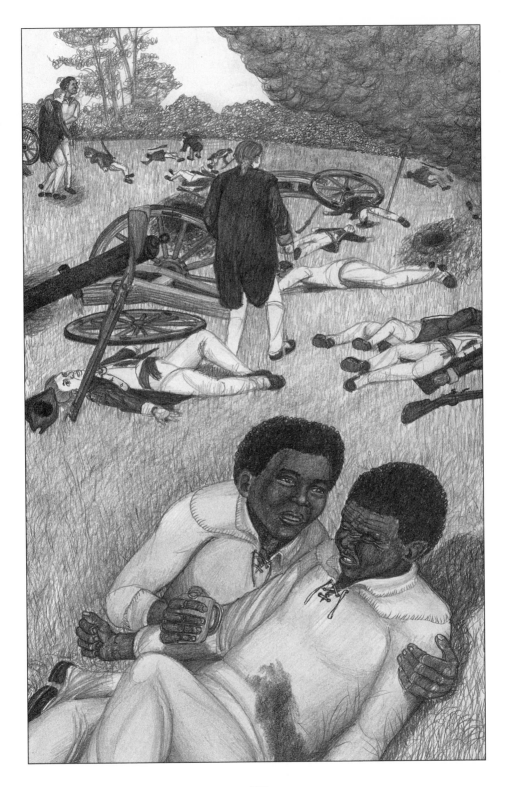

Cuff became. He found that wooden sticks worked well as crutches and that talking gently to a wounded man could help calm him down.

When he went to the stream to refill his canteen, the water was red—blood red. Cuff turned away sick. He couldn't fill his canteen with that. He'd just try to help as much as he could without water.

After several hours, Cuff lost count of how many men he had helped back to camp or hoisted onto a cart. But no matter how many he helped, more kept coming.

As he listened for another cry, Cuff came across Nat standing over a bloody soldier. "I know I'm dying," the man was saying in a raspy voice. "I have to tell you . . . tomorrow . . . you must get those Hessians for me." His voice became a whisper. "I saw my wife today . . . our doorway . . . could see them threatening her . . . couldn't get to her . . . too many . . . we had to retreat." They could hardly hear his last few words as he died. Nat vomited as Cuff cried next to him. The two boys hugged each other close.

"These men are all dead," Nat whispered. "We can't help them anymore. Let's go." As they returned to camp, they said silent prayers through their tears. They knew that what they saw that day would be imprinted in their minds forever.

The smell of smoke and blood was everywhere—even back at the American camp. Food had been sent down from Butts Hill. No one took pleasure in eating, although they ate hungrily.

"Did we lose many men?" Cuff asked, as they lay on their blankets, trying to get some sleep.

"Only two," Jack whispered. "Seven men injured."

"That's all?" Cuff asked, amazed. With all the injured and dead he had seen, it was remarkable that his regiment—his brothers—hadn't suffered more.

"Do you think we'll have to fight again tomorrow?" Cuff asked.

"They're still out there, and we're still here," Big John said.

No one else spoke—each man haunted by the memories of the day. *We're all lucky to be alive*, Cuff thought. He hoped he could say the same when the war was finally over.

TEN

"WAKE UP, CUFF!" CUFF OPENED HIS eyes and saw Nat staring down at him. The first hint of light was in the sky and a steady rain was falling. "We've been ordered to bring in the rest of the wounded," Nat said, "and to keep at it unless we see signs of the enemy."

Cuff rubbed his eyes. He had been dreaming about going to see his family. He'd been walking up a dirt path to a door. Behind the door, he knew, was his mother, father, and brother. Just as he lifted the latch, Nat had woken him up.

"Are you all right?" Nat asked, looking closely at his friend.

"Yes," Cuff nodded. "But I'm not looking forward to another day near that bloody brook." He shivered.

"We have no choice . . . we're not free yet, Cuff," Nat said. "But the water's probably running clear by now."

Cuff shook his head. "I'll remember what it looked like yesterday, for as long as I live."

By dawn, the men of the First Rhode Island Regiment were back in the valley, tending the wounded and dead just as they had the day before. As they worked, cannon fire sounded in the distance.

The British were shooting from Turkey Hill and the other side of Quaker Hill, and the Americans were shooting from Butts Hill. With every blast, Cuff wondered if they'd be ordered to battle again. In a way, he didn't know what was worse—fighting strong and healthy men or tending the dead and the wounded. Helping to bury thirty men in a single grave left everyone silent and numb.

In the early evening, one of Major Ward's aides called everyone together outside the major's tent. When the major himself stepped out of his tent, every soldier saluted.

"At ease," the major said, gesturing for the men to sit down on the ground. He sat on a chair in the center. "These past two days have been difficult but especially so for you. It was your first battle, and I know you've been assigned some of the hardest tasks."

Cuff closed his eyes, thinking of all the dead and disfigured he had seen.

"You performed well," the major continued. "This morning, General Sullivan praised the First Rhode Island Regiment. He called you heroes in this battle for justice and freedom and asked that you be told some important things." The major caught Cuff's eye and nodded. "For one, yesterday's battle was declared an American victory. We drove the enemy back on all fronts, inflicting almost twice as many casualties as we suffered. That's why they decided not to attack today. In fact, it's reported that the Hessian commander you defeated yesterday requested a transfer. He thought his men would refuse, if ordered to fight you again today."

Some of the men cheered.

Cuff looked at Nat. "It's good news, but somehow I don't feel like cheering," he whispered.

"I don't either," Nat whispered back. "I'm just relieved not to have to fight again."

"Two weeks ago," Major Ward continued, "it seemed that we'd be able to drive the British from Newport and win back this important island. But now, with our ranks nearly half of what they were and without a navy to aid us, we must retreat to the mainland."

Cuff's heart began to race, and he thought of his family. He was almost sure they were on the mainland. *Will they be hard to find?* he wondered. He had to force his attention back to Major Ward.

"We'll be striking some of the tents on Butts Hill after dark. That doesn't give us much time. Some of the artillery and heavy supplies have already been taken across on Howland's Ferry. The rest of it will be brought to the ferry landing on carts. The First Rhode Island Regiment has been assigned as rear guard to cover the retreat. You'll each be issued extra ammunition this evening, and follow the same procedure as when we left the siege lines at Newport. Hope the enemy doesn't realize what we're up to. You'll cross the Sakonnet in flatboats." With that, the major stood up. Everyone else stood too and saluted.

"You're good men, all of you," Major Ward said, with a smile. "I'm very proud of you." He dismissed everyone except for Cuff and Nat, whom he needed to deliver messages.

"Howland's Ferry goes to Tiverton," Cuff said to Nat as they waited outside Major Ward's tent. "I remember Mr. Barker saying the Beckhams and my family might have crossed that way to the mainland."

"They probably did," Nat said. "That, or Bristol Ferry."

"I sure wish I knew where my family was," Cuff said shaking his head. "As great as it will be to get my freedom, I know I won't be happy until I find them."

"That's how I feel too," Nat said. "My mama is all alone. At least your family's together."

*   *   *

That night, under the dark, star-filled sky, the First Rhode Island Regiment began its retreat. Cuff and Nat walked side by side, both exhausted from their long day. Everyone was silent, listening closely for sounds from the enemy.

"I sure hope we get there soon," Cuff whispered to Nat. "This quiet is making me nervous. Do you think the British know we're moving?"

"Probably not," Nat whispered back. "Otherwise we would have already heard cannon fire. I think we're pretty close to the ferry."

Suddenly, the men in front of them halted, the sound of galloping hooves becoming louder. As the horse came close, Major Ward lit a torch and stood in the middle of the road. The horse came to a quick stop, and its rider quickly dismounted.

"It's General Lafayette," Cuff whispered to Nat

with surprise. He gazed with admiration at the young Frenchman in the torchlight.

Major Ward saluted the young marquis. "You've made good time from Boston," he said. "I didn't expect you back so soon."

"That I have," General Lafayette said, "but not quick enough to help in the fighting. I'm returning with news that'll be useless to you now. The fleet couldn't sail. They said they'd send men by land. But I heard you performed very well without the French Navy."

"We did, indeed, sir. Thank you, sir," Major Ward said.

"I've come to see you to the ferry," said General Lafayette. "Is there anyone else behind you?"

"No sir, we're the last," Major Ward said, looking around at his men. "And, fortunately, we've seen no sign of the enemy."

"Good," General Lafayette said, approvingly. "Nobody else has either." He mounted his horse and rode back in the direction he'd come, alongside Major Ward.

"That's really something," Nat murmured to Cuff. "The Marquis de Lafayette stayed with the Americans until the end."

Cuff nodded, smiling. He had known the marquis was a good man from the time they first met.

Before long they were at the waters of the Sakonnet, preparing to cross on flatboats. Cuff remembered his second day in the Continental Army when Nat had shown him the boats he had helped make. It seemed like ages ago.

As they boarded the small boats, Cuff looked back at the silent, dark land behind him. "You know," he said to Nat. "I've never been off the island before. I wonder if I'll ever be back?"

ELEVEN

"ISN'T IT GREAT, CUFF? NO SMOKE BURNING our eyes, no cannons booming." Nat threw his head back to smell the air of Tiverton. It had been two days since the Battle of Rhode Island had ended.

"I suppose," Cuff said, pressing his bare toes into the warm sand of the beach. "I still can't believe I'm looking at Aquidneck Island instead of standing on it." He knew he'd miss the rocky terrain of Barker's Hill and the farm around it. Never again would he spend a quiet Sunday visiting his mother, father, and brother on Beckham's farm.

"Just looking up there makes me feel safe," Nat said, turning around and looking up.

Cuff followed Nat's gaze, high up on a cliff of the mainland. There he saw a long row of cannons aimed toward Aquidneck Island. And on the walls of the new Tiverton Heights Fort was another battery. "I guess I'd rather be here than there," he said. "I wonder what they have planned for us today—or even next week."

"Couldn't be any better than yesterday," Nat answered. "Washing up in the bay and eating a real meal was quite a treat."

The rattle of drums brought them both to their feet. "Well, I'm off to drill," Nat said.

"I'll be joining you in a couple of days," Cuff said, pulling on his socks and boots. "Major Ward said a shipment of muskets is coming in for the new recruits. I'll be training with them."

"Now that we weren't able to take Newport, I wonder how much longer the war will go on?" Nat asked as they hurried back to the new camp.

"I hope it isn't much longer," Cuff said, shaking his head. "All this fighting is taking quite a toll on the island."

When they reached the fork in the road, the two young men locked hands in a long, firm shake. Then Nat headed toward the field where the drills were to be held, and Cuff headed toward Major Ward's tent, which he had helped to set up the day before.

"Ah, there you are, private," Major Ward said when Cuff arrived. With no smoke filling the air, the white tent walls seemed brighter than usual. "Take this message up to General Sullivan, and wait for a reply."

"Yes, sir," Cuff said, saluting.

Several horses were grazing outside of General Sullivan's tent. At the doorway as Cuff gave his message to an aide, a stocky man in civilian clothes came out of the tent. Cuff's eyes lit up with recognition.

"Say there!" the man said, looking at him with surprise. "It's Cuff from Paradise Farm."

"Mr. Barker!" Cuff exclaimed with amazement, recognizing Silas Barker, the brother of his former owner.

"Aye, lad. What luck to find you here. I thought

I'd have to search the whole camp. It's good to see you healthy and in one piece," he said, putting an arm around Cuff's shoulders and walking him a few paces from the tent. "Been through some terrible times, I hear."

"No worse than anyone else around here, sir," Cuff said, humbly.

"Well, I've got a bit of good news," Silas said. "My brother wanted you to know that the Beckhams are safe and settled in Millville, up in Massachusetts. Your ma, pa, and little brother are safe with them."

Cuff beamed as the tension drained out of him. "Oh, that is good news!" he exclaimed, ready to dance with delight. "Thank you, sir! Thank you!" Suddenly, he frowned. "So Mr. Barker knows I'm here?" he asked.

"Oh, yes, lad," Silas said. "His wife was doing his bidding when she sent you off. That British colonel was getting pushy about having you on his staff, I hear."

"Are they all right after the siege and all?" Cuff asked with concern. "The Continental lines went right to the hill."

"Last I heard they were fine," Silas said, frowning. "I haven't had much contact with them, of course."

"That packet for Officer Chapin will be ready in just a minute, Mr. Barker," General Sullivan's aide called from the tent.

"That'll be fine," Silas said. "I can wait." He turned away from Cuff to light his pipe.

My family is safe! Cuff thought in a happy daze.

But one thing confused him. Why would Mr. Barker send him to the Continental Army if he was a Tory?

"Look at this!" Cuff recognized General Sullivan's blustery voice coming from the tent. "Chapin sent us all the details of the British fleet that put into Newport yesterday—from the number of cannon to the condition of the sails. General Clinton himself has taken up quarters in Newport with 4,500 more troops."

"We got our troops off the island just in time," said the aide.

"Yes indeed," said General Sullivan. "I don't know how Chapin does it. As always, his information is up-to-date. And from where he is on Little Compton, he can't even see Newport."

"His best view of the island is that big rocky hill," the aide offered. "The signals come from there."

The rocky hill, thought Cuff. Suddenly it all made sense. The big, rocky hill across from Little Compton was Barker's Hill. Mr. Barker wasn't a Tory at all! He had only pretended to side with the British so he could send information to the Americans.

He knew he was right when Silas winked at him. He wanted to know more, but it wasn't the time to ask questions.

"Whoever the spy is, he's doing a great job," General Sullivan said. "Why, he even got us information that the French Navy was leaving the bay on August 10th—nearly a day before our couriers brought the news from Warwick."

Cuff remembered when that had happened—he

had been on top of Barker's hill the afternoon before he was sent to the army. Mr. Barker must have been spying, Cuff realized, remembering how his former owner used to pace back and forth on top of the hill. What else could he have been doing? How could he have sent a message? The only thing up there was the stone wall and the gate to the sheep pasture. *That must be it! The rails and crossbars of the gate! That's why, after four years, he suddenly didn't want me up there. He was afraid I'd mess up some code.*

Cuff was thrilled to discover all of this, and relieved to learn that Mr. Barker wasn't a Loyalist.

"Something tells me you understand now," Silas said in a low tone.

"I think I do," Cuff said, proud to have figured it out himself.

"You're a smart lad, Cuff," Silas said. "I trust you can keep secrets, too."

"I certainly can," Cuff smiled.

General Sullivan came out of his tent. "Private, here's the reply for Major Ward," he said, handing Cuff a sealed note.

"Yes sir!" Cuff said, saluting. He grinned at Silas Barker before running off, feeling very special. After all, he knew something that even General Sullivan didn't know. And he was certain that his family was safe. He couldn't wait to tell Nat. *Now I have to get good at this soldiering*, he thought. *So we can get this war over with.*

AFTERWORD

Soon after the Battle of Rhode Island, the First Rhode Island Regiment was ordered back to East Greenwich, Rhode Island, where Cuff and Nat learned more about soldiering and helping protect Narragansett Bay. They moved to Newport after the British left in 1779, and were quartered in a building that had been used as the slave-trading center. Colonel Christopher Greene was commander of the regiment, with the ranks swelling to nearly 200 men. Not all of them were African American.

During the next three years, the regiment took part in several significant battles, including the siege of Yorktown in Virginia during the summer and early fall of 1781. The regiment returned to New York State and remained active until the summer of 1783, when they were released from duty. The slaves who had served were allowed to pursue their lives as free men.